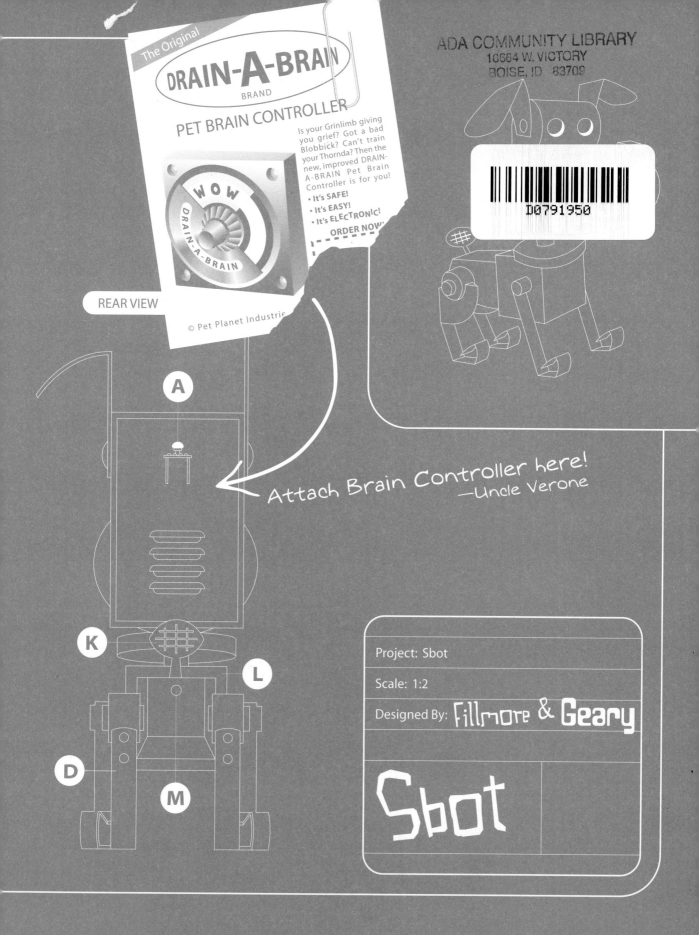

The Original

DRAIN-A-BRAIN
BRAND

PET BRAIN CONTROLLER

Is your Grinlimb giving you grief? Got a bad Blobbick? Can't train your Thornda? Then the new, improved DRAIN-A-BRAIN Pet Brain Controller is for you!

• It's SAFE!
• It's EASY!
• It's ELECTRONIC!

ORDER NOW!

WOW
DRAIN-A-BRAIN

REAR VIEW

© Pet Planet Industries

A

Attach Brain Controller here!
—Uncle Verone

K

L

D

M

Project: Sbot

Scale: 1:2

Designed By: Fillmore & Geary

Sbot

FILLMORE & GEARY

TAKE OFF!

written by
MARK SHULMAN

designed and illustrated by
PHILLIP FICKLING

chronicle books · san francisco

Fillmore and Geary

were just like you and your best friend, except for a couple of things.

They weren't from Earth. They had a flying scooter. One of them was a robot. And they always made their beds.

Other than that, there was really no difference at all.

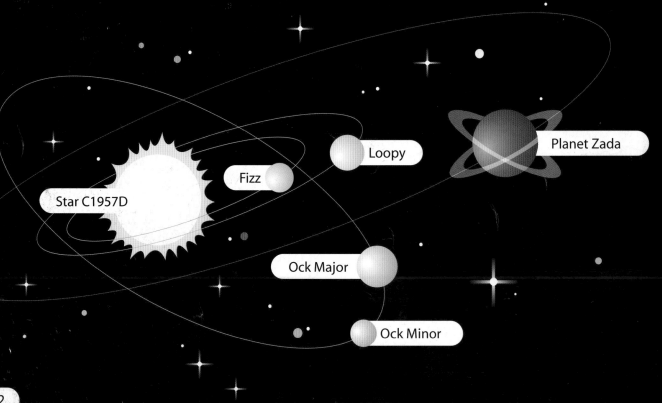

Loopy

Planet Zada

Fizz

Star C1957D

Ock Major

Ock Minor

Great Winged Thornda

The boys had everything boys need. What they didn't need was a pet. So of course, that's what they wanted. But on Planet Zada, having a pet was like having a bad dream. You didn't want to wake up with one.

Planet Zada was a quadrillion and thirteen miles from Earth. But it still got excellent TV reception.

The boys were watching an old TV show from some faraway planet when they saw their first dog.

"Look at that boy's pet," Geary said in his buzzy voice. "It catches balls. It chases sticks. It saves little girls who get stuck in elevators."

Fillmore was convinced. They needed a dog more than anything. And that's why Uncle Verone gave them the keys to his Invention Room.

Uncle Verone

Keys to Invention Room

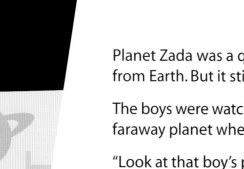

Earth Dog

Television

The boys knew as much about dogs as *you* know about fixing rockets. But they ignored that little fact and built a dog anyway.

As soon as they were done, they hurried to the garage, where Uncle Verone was fixing the family rocket. "Who's your new friend?" he asked.

"First we named him Super Dog Robot," explained Fillmore. "Then it got shorter, to SuperBot. Now it's just Sbot."

Uncle Verone was delighted. "Welcome to the family, Sbot. It's time to power you up."

Body

Leg-O-Lator

Body and Legs

ROBOHEAD

Body, Legs, and Head

Rollers

Conveyor Belt

U-Slide

Safety Goggles

Sbot

Laser

9

Power Cable

Chain

Geary flipped the switch. There was a sound like metal peas in a blender. Then Sbot's eyes lit up. His tail wagged, just a little, and then it stopped. Finally, Sbot got up to shake hands—*on two legs*!

"How do you do?" said a very polite Sbot. He looked around. "Waking up has made me tired. Where's my room?" Then he left for the kitchen to drink their best motor oil.

Nobody spoke for a while, until Fillmore said, "Hey Geary, he thinks he's a robot just like you."

"He's NOT a robot!" snapped Geary, feeling jealous. "He's just a very bad dog."

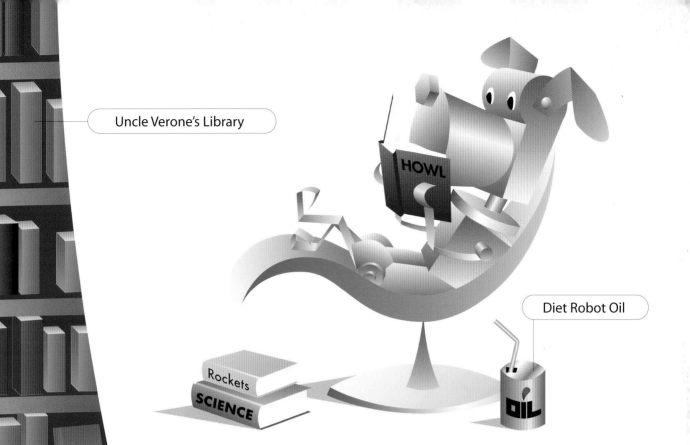

Uncle Verone's Library

Diet Robot Oil

HOWL

Rockets

SCIENCE

OIL

In the library, Uncle Verone explained the problem.

"Sbot can't act like real dogs until he meets some. I've found five planets on the Super Map that have dogs on them." Then he smiled. "How would you boys like to take the rocket on a little adventure?"

The boys loved an adventure. They packed and packed and packed the rocket with so much very important stuff, nobody knew for sure if it would take off.

"Why don't I stay home?" Sbot offered. "Dogs protect the house, right? I could call the police if anything happens."

"Nice try, Sbot," said Geary, as he pressed the starter. The rocket roared to life. Fillmore grabbed both armrests, excited but a little scared to go so far away from his uncle.

"See you at dinnertime!" called Uncle Verone, waving as the rocket vanished beyond the clouds.

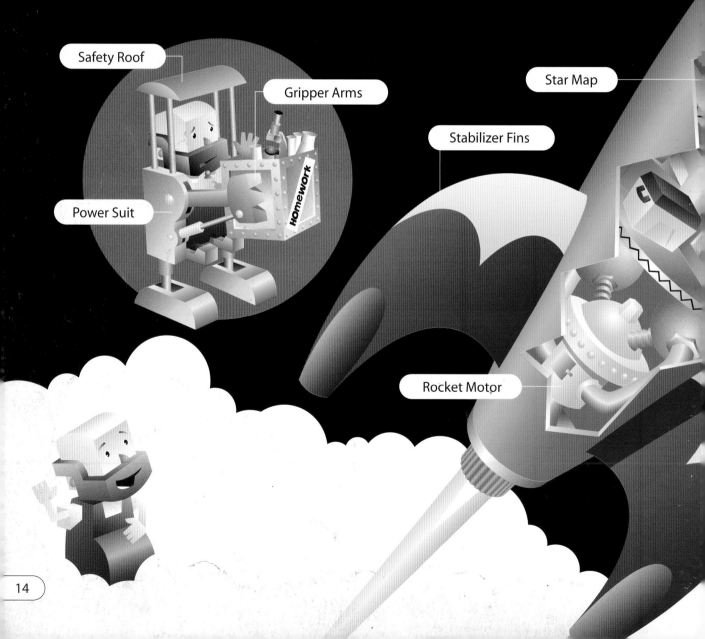

Safety Roof

Gripper Arms

Star Map

Stabilizer Fins

Power Suit

Rocket Motor

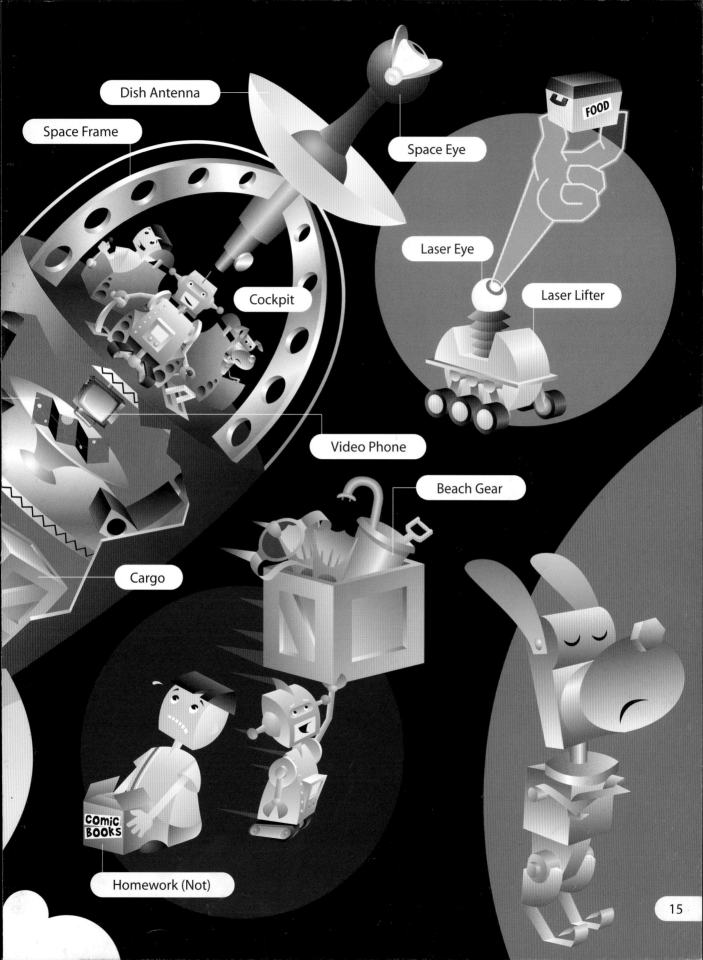

Dish Antenna

Space Frame

Space Eye

Laser Eye

Laser Lifter

Cockpit

Video Phone

Beach Gear

Cargo

Homework (Not)

Zero Gravity

DOGS A-Z

View Port

Sbot was reading all about dogs. "You want ME to act like THIS?" He couldn't believe it. "But they're so . . . so . . . "

"So much *fun*," said Geary.

"Look, Sbot," joked Fillmore, "if we'd wanted you to be human, we wouldn't need Geary." Geary zapped Fillmore with his laser finger.

Sbot pointed to the small gadget on the back of his head. "What's this?" he asked.

The boys were too busy practicing zero-gravity somersaults and laughing to answer. Soon enough, Geary asked Sbot to land the rocket. "Like a good dog."

Pet Brain Controller

WOW

DRAIN-A-BRAIN

On Planet One, dogs were everywhere: on the sidewalks, on the streets, and on the telephone. On the telephone?

"These dogs act just like Sbot," complained Fillmore. "Where's the *woof-woof?*" Geary was too busy taking pictures to answer.

Sbot liked this planet just fine. He bought a pair of sunglasses and some postcards. But the parking meter was about to expire, so they had to go.

SAVINGS AND BONE

Bank

Banker

Street Vendor

19

Planet Two was only a half-billion miles away. They arrived before lunch. The jungle planet trembled. Huge heads panted with joy.

"Get your doggy dinosaur breath away from me," yelled Fillmore as he ran.

"Watch out for the tongue!" cried Geary. It was almost too late, but Sbot swooped down with the rocket just in time.

"Hop in!" he said, and the boys hopped. Except for a drool bath, no one was hurt.

Dog's Ear

Flea Plant

Scottisaurus

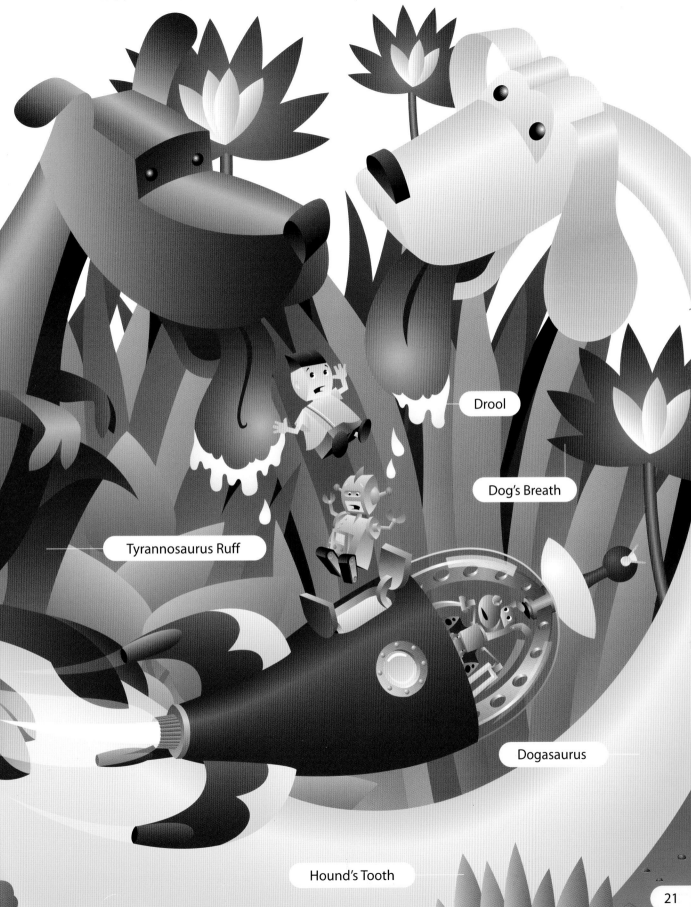

Drool

Dog's Breath

Tyrannosaurus Ruff

Dogasaurus

Hound's Tooth

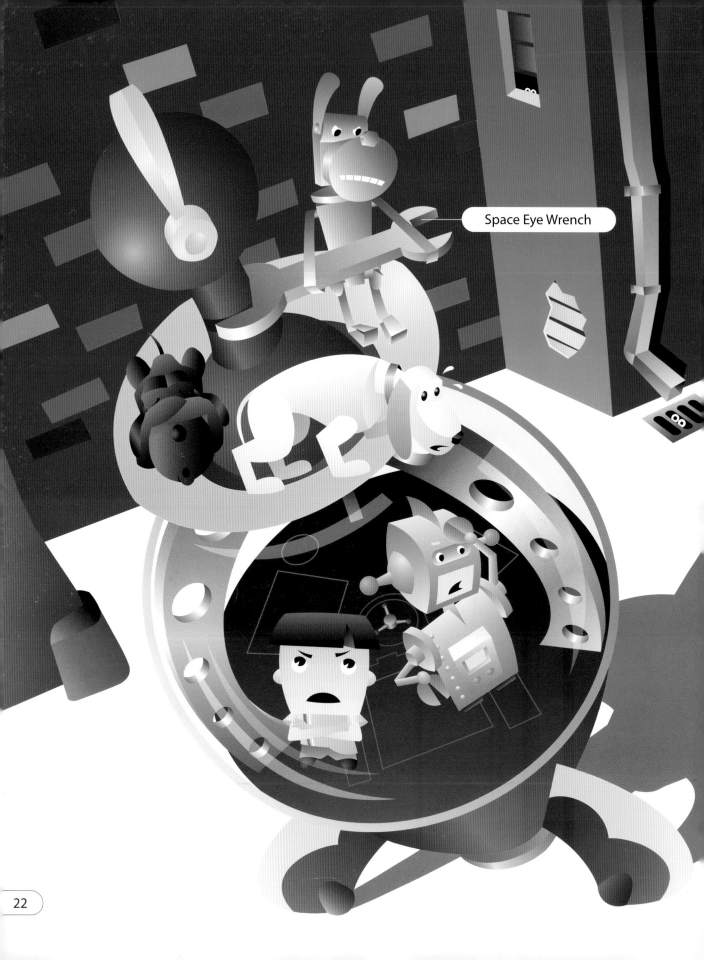

Space Eye Wrench

Secret Dog Hiding Place

"Oh, great," said Geary after they crashed on Planet Three. "The dogs act like cats and the cats act like dogs. Which ones do we want Sbot to act like?"

"He should act like a Fix-It Robot," said Fillmore. "Or else we'll never get out of here."

"Only two more planets," Sbot whispered to himself.

Volcano

Snapping Jaw

Mean Dog

Ancient Bone

24

Maybe the snapping, snarling wolf-dogs on Planet Four could bite through robot metal. Maybe not.

But nobody wanted to find out.

Sbot commanded the rocket through fire and volcanoes. "Hang on!" he ordered, and they bolted quickly to deep space.

Fire Pit

The mission was failing. The boys were miserable. The soup was cold.

But Sbot was happily zigzagging the ship between comets. He was certain he'd soon be back in the library with Uncle Verone.

"Uncle Verone!" shouted Fillmore into the old videophone." Should we just give up?"

"Open your eyes," said Uncle Verone through the static. "The answer is usually right in front of you." Then he said, "Maybe it's on that funny-looking blue planet you're about to smash into!"

The Moon

Space Junk

Blue Planet

Mars

Planet Five was funny looking all right, but they didn't smash into it. Sbot slowed down just in time. Geary checked the Superscope for signs of life on the planet.

"Hmmm," he said. "I see a big city. There are fish in the water, birds in the air, people on the ground, alligators in the sewers, pigeons on the statues, and . . . DOGS!"

Fillmore was jumping up and down with excitement, making every sound he thought dogs made. *"Arf! Arf! Meow! Moo!"*

Sbot was certain this was just another silly planet. But he was doggone wrong.

Brooklyn Bridge

Empire State Building

Chrysler Building

Tour Boat

Statue of Liberty

Charge Meter

E F

RECHARGE YOUR
BATTERY PARK

Finally the boys had found the right kind of dogs: big and small, fast and slow, wet and smelly. "Make nice!" commanded Geary in his dog-trainer voice.

Sbot muttered and joined in. "Look!" said Fillmore. "The Drain-A-Brain is working! Sbot's starting to act like the other dogs."

"Yeah," said Geary. "Once the dial goes from WOW to BOW-WOW, his brain will roll over and play dead."

Sbot barked. Sbot whined. He nearly had a doggy mind. The dial turned a bit, making a faint *ticking* sound.

Sbot chased his tail. The dogs chased Sbot. The boys watched. "Is this all they do?" asked Geary. *Tick.*

Sbot drooled. The dial moved a little faster. Fillmore noticed something on his shoe. He didn't like it at all. *Tick.*

Sbot rolled over. "He sure was good at fixing rockets," said Geary. *Tick. Tick.*

Sbot sniffed a Scottie's bottom. "I guess you'll have to fly us home," said Fillmore. *Tick. Tick.*

Geary looked at Fillmore. Fillmore looked at Geary. *Tick. Tick. Tick. Tick.*

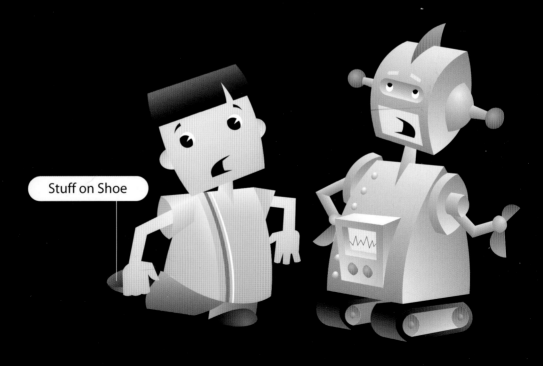

Stuff on Shoe

THE DIAL!

They both jumped for it at the same time and *slammmed* it back to the other side.

Fire Hydrant

Drooling Tongue

The trip back seemed to go very quickly, especially with Sbot doing the driving. The boys had more important things to think about, like new inventions. And dinner.

"Now remember, Sbot," said Geary, "I'm still the only robot. And sometimes you have to be the dog, okay?" Sbot chuckled and nodded.

"Talk like a dog again, Sbot," said Fillmore.

"*Arf! Arf! Meow! Moo!*" said Sbot with a smile. And with his front leg, he turned the spaceship toward home.

Joystick

Back on Planet Zada, everyone was happy.

Whenever the boys asked nicely, Sbot was glad to chase sticks or roll over or shake hands without saying, "How do you do?" But most of the time, he fixed machines and worked with Uncle Verone inventing things.

They were finishing the plans for a giant submarine when Fillmore and Geary burst into the garage. The boys had just built a cat.

"Speak," said Geary.

"*Woof,*" said the cat.

Pencil Controller

Submarine Plans

Auto Pencil

THE END

For Kara, who believed in my stories—*Mark*

To my brother Tony, who believed in me—*Phil*

Copyright © 2004 by Phillip Fickling and Mark Shulman.
All rights reserved.

Art, design, and paper engineering by Phillip Fickling.
Story and text by Mark Shulman.
Edited by Andrea Spooner.
The artwork for this book was prepared by using Macromedia Freehand 10.
Manufactured in Hong Kong.

Read & Build Books is a trademark of Phillip Fickling and Mark Shulman.
Created at Oomf, Inc. *www.Oomf.com*

Library of Congress Cataloging-in-Publication Data available.
ISBN 1-58717-256-9

Distributed in Canada by Raincoast Books
9050 Shaughnessy Street, Vancouver, British Columbia V6P 6E5

10 9 8 7 6 5 4 3 2 1

Chronicle Books LLC
85 Second Street, San Francisco, California 94105

www.chroniclekids.com

Mark Shulman

Mark writes for children and adults. His books include *How I Built Rusty, Secret Hiding Places,* and *Attack of the Killer Video Book.* Mark is also a sometimes tour guide in New York City, and he knows full well that the Empire State Building and the Chrysler Building are wandering around on page 28. Mark (left) lives with Hannah (right) and Kara (not pictured) in a building the size of the Titanic (also not pictured).

Phillip Fickling

Phillip and his wife, Jenny, live on the south island of New Zealand in a bright blue house. Their art studio is kind of like Uncle Verone's Invention Room: lots of computers, robots, submarines, and other things that are top secret. Phillip is a highly-respected inventor and paper engineer, as you can also see on projects like *How I Built Rusty.* He does most of his work on a computer and likes a nap in the afternoon. Thinking is hard work!